If I Ran the School

8:00 - 10:00 Gym
10:00 - 12:00 Art
12:00 - 2:00 Lunch
2:00 - 3:00 Recess

24 Funny School Poems
Selected and Introduced by

Bruce Lansky

"King of Giggle Poetry"

Scholastic Inc.

New York • Toronto • London • Auckland • Sydney
Mexico City • New Delhi • Hong Kong • Buenos Aires

Cover illustration by
Stephen Carpenter

Interior illustrations by
Stephen Carpenter and Mike Gordon

ISBN 0-439-82595-4

12 11 10 9 8 7 6 5 4 3 2 1   5 6 7 8 9 10/0

Printed in the U.S.A.
First printing, September 2005

The only thing I remember about kindergarten is building tall towers with blocks, pouring water from one container into another, and being in love with my teacher.

Second grade (I skipped first grade) was very different from kindergarten. There were no more blocks and water containers. Instead, there was reading, writing, arithmetic, and homework. Until then, I thought "homework" was work you did at home, like making your bed. I didn't know "homework" also meant reading books, writing book reports, and studying spelling words.

Because my mom was a school librarian, I read books at home for fun and gave her a "report" before she returned them to the library. So, it didn't seem much like work to read books for school and write reports about them. Since I enjoyed reading, I also found spelling easy. (Although, there are certain words I still wonder how to spell, like *necessary* and *recommend*. Did I spell them right?)

I've written some new poems about school, which I included in this book along with other poems by some of my favorite poets. Whenever I read them, I get a big smile on my face. I hope you do, too!

Bruce Lansky

P.S. If I ran the school, I'd invite Ben and Jerry to scoop ice cream in the lunchroom, and I'd invite my favorite authors to visit. What would *you* do if you ran the school?

Minnetonka, MN
September 2005

I Can't Wait for Summer

I can't wait for summer, when school days are done,
to spend the days playing outside in the sun.
I won't have to study. No homework, no tests.
Just afternoons spent on adventures and quests.

Instead of mathematics and writing reports,
I'll go to the park and play summertime sports.
Instead of assignments, report cards, and grades,
I'll get to play baseball and watch the parades.

I'll swing on the playground. I'll swim in the pool
instead of just practicing lessons in school.
The second the school year is finally done
I'll spend every minute with friends having fun.

I hardly can wait for the end of the year.
I'm counting the days until summer is here.
It's hard to be patient. It's hard to be cool.
It's hard to believe it's the first day of school.

Kenn Nesbitt

I'm Getting Sick of Peanut Butter

I look inside my lunchbox,
and, oh, what do I see?
A peanut butter sandwich
staring glumly back at me.

I know I had one yesterday,
and, yes, the day before.
In fact, that's all I've eaten
for at least a month or more.

I'm sure tomorrow afternoon
the outlook's just as bleak.
I'll bet I'm having peanut butter
every day this week.

I'm getting sick of peanut butter
sandwiches for lunch.
Why can't I have baloney
or potato chips to munch?

I wish I had lasagna
or a piece of pumpkin pie.
Another day of peanut butter
might just make me cry.

But still this awful sandwich
is in every lunch I take.
You see, it is the only thing
my mom knows how to make.

Kenn Nesbitt

Bring Your Own Lunch

Don't eat school lunches—
not even a lick.
They might make you nauseous.
They might make you sick.

Just take a small bite and
you'll start to feel ill.
If the veggies don't get you,
the meatloaf sure will.

Bruce Lansky

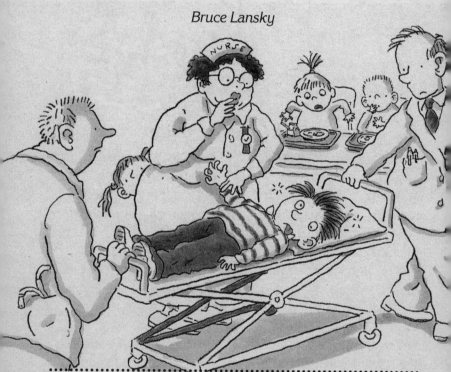

The Story Behind the Poem: When I visit schools, I'm often offered a free lunch in the cafeteria. In some schools, the food is a lot better than I would expect. But in others, I take one look, then suggest to the principal that we "Go out for lunch."

Afterschool Snack

Right now I'm kinda hungry, dude.
The 'frigerator's full of food.
There's meat loaf and a chicken wing
And half a turkey sandwich-thing.

There's day-old tuna, almost new,
Some Tupperware with potluck stew,
Some leftover spaghetti sauce,
And wilted salad partly tossed.

There's also Jell-O (sort of green),
A chunk of cheese, a lima bean,
A jar of pickles, can of soup,
And something best described as goop.

There's broccoli that's growing old,
A loaf of bread that's growing mold...
The 'frigerator's full, but hey—
There's nothing that I want today.

Neal Levin

What I Found in My Desk

A ripe peach with an ugly bruise,
a pair of stinky tennis shoes,
a day-old ham-and-cheese on rye,
a swimsuit that I left to dry,
a pencil that glows in the dark,
some bubble gum found in the park,
a paper bag with cookie crumbs,
an old kazoo that barely hums,
a spelling test I almost failed,
a letter that I should have mailed,
and one more thing, I must confess,
a note from teacher: Clean This Mess!!!!

Bruce Lansky

The Story Behind the Poem: I've always been a pack rat who doesn't throw anything out. That's why my school desk was completely gross. I got many notes from teachers to "Clean This Mess."

When the Teacher Isn't Looking

When the teacher's back is turned,
we never scream and shout.
Never do we drop our books
and try to freak her out.

No one throws a pencil
at the ceiling of the class.
No one tries to hit the fire alarm
and break the glass.

We don't cough in unison
and loudly clear our throats.
No one's shooting paper wads
or passing little notes.

She must think we're so polite.
We never make a peep.
Really, though, it's just because
we all go right to sleep.

Kenn Nesbitt

9

I Ripped My Pants at School Today

I ripped my pants at school today
while going down the slide.
It wasn't just a little tear
I ripped 'em open wide.

Now everyone at school can see
my purple underwear.
Although the sight makes people laugh
I'm glad I've got them there.

Robert Pottle

I'm Practicing Telepathy

I'm practicing telepathy.
I'm learning ESP.
I'm getting mental images
like pictures on TV.

I thought I'd pick your brain a bit.
I thought I'd read your mind
to get the answers to this test,
but now I'm in a bind.

I probed your thoughts and consciousness,
and now I guarantee,
we both are gonna flunk
because you're copying from me.

Kenn Nesbitt

I Should Have Studied

I didn't study for the test
and now I'm feeling blue.
I copied off your paper
and I flunked it just like you.

Bruce Lansky

The Story Behind the Poem: I was a pretty good student, so cheating didn't make any sense for two reasons: One, I knew cheating was wrong. Two, I knew most kids in class weren't likely to have better answers on their tests than I had!

Fs Are "Fabulous"

Hey, Mom and Dad! I got my grades!
And you'll be thrilled to hear
the marks on our report cards
are changed around this year.

A bunch of kids were telling me
this morning on the bus,
that they had heard some teachers say
that Fs are "fabulous."

And Ds are proudly given out
for work that's "dynamite."
They're used to honor kids like me,
whose brains are really bright.

So C of course is super "cool"—
I've got a few of those.
I wish they could be Ds and Fs,
but that's the way it goes.

I'm pleased to see my teacher
didn't give an A or B.
I've worked too hard for one of those.
Gosh, aren't you proud of me?

I see you don't believe me.
You think that I am lying?
At least you will agree
that I should get an A for trying!

Ted Scheu

DVD Report

When your book report is due,
here's a helpful little clue:
If you haven't read the book,
rent the movie—have a look.
Don't forget the special feature;
you'll find stuff to thrill your teacher.
Actors talking 'bout the plot—
that should help you out a lot.
Your report will be real groovy...
unless the book's not like the movie.

Bruce Lansky

The Story Behind the Poem: DVDs didn't exist when I was a kid, but sometimes we could go to the theater to watch a film version of a book. The problem was the same then as it is now: What if they changed the story when they made the movie?

My Teacher Loves Her iPod

My teacher loves her iPod.
It's always in her ear.
She doesn't mind it if we joke
or chat 'cause she can't hear.

If we don't pay attention,
she doesn't seem to care.
Whenever she has music on,
she wears a distant stare.

Our principal dropped by one day,
and she paid no attention.
He took away her iPod
and sent her to detention.

Bruce Lansky

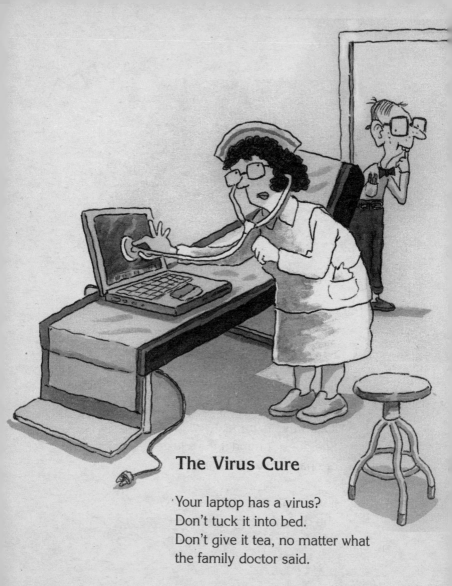

The Virus Cure

Your laptop has a virus?
Don't tuck it into bed.
Don't give it tea, no matter what
the family doctor said.

Don't take it to the school nurse.
Don't rest it for a week.
The only way to cure it is to
show it to a geek.

Bruce Lansky

Camera Phone

I tried to take a photo of the
girl who sits behind me.
I think she is so pretty that
I want it to remind me.

Instead the picture that I took
with my new cell phone camera—
was a photo of my ear
and not of my friend, Tamra.

Bruce Lansky

The Story Behind the Poem: I'm not too clever with technology.
The first time I snapped a photo with a camera phone, I took a
picture of my ear. *No kidding!*

Homework, I Love You

Homework, I love you. I think that you're great.
It's wonderful fun when you keep me up late.
I think you're the best when I'm totally stressed,
preparing and cramming all night for a test.

Homework, I love you. What more can I say?
I love to do hundreds of problems each day.
You boggle my mind and you make me go blind,
but still I'm ecstatic that you were assigned.

Homework, I love you. I tell you, it's true.
There's nothing more fun or exciting to do.
You're never a chore, for it's you I adore.
I wish that our teacher would hand you out more.

Homework, I love you. You thrill me inside.
I'm filled with emotions. I'm fit to be tied.
I cannot complain when you frazzle my brain.
Of course, that's because I'm completely insane.

Kenn Nesbitt

Too Busy

I've folded all my laundry
and put it in the drawer.
I've changed my linen, made my bed,
and swept my bedroom floor.

I've emptied out the garbage
and fixed tomorrow's lunch.
I've baked some cookies for dessert
and given dad a munch.

I've searched the house for pencils
and sharpened every one.
There are so many things to do
when homework must be done.

Bruce Lansky

The Story Behind the Poem: Putting stuff like homework off till the last moment was a big problem for me in school. Strangely enough, as an adult, I rarely put off work matters, but I've managed to avoid cleaning the garage for years!

How to Torture Your Teacher

Only raise your hand when
you want to sharpen your pencil
or go to the bathroom.
Repeat every ten minutes.

Never raise your hand
when you want to answer a question;
instead, yell, "Oooh! Oooh! Oooh!"
and then, when the teacher calls on you,
say, "I forgot what I was going to say."

Lean your chair back,
take off your shoes, and
put your feet up on your desk.
Act surprised when the teacher
puts all four legs of your chair back on the floor.

Drop the eraser end of your pencil
on your desk.
See how high it will bounce.

Drop your books on the floor.
See how loud a noise you can make.

The Story Behind the Poem: When I visit schools, kids ask
me to read this poem most often. If I get the okay from the
teacher, I pick nine students to read it—one student per stanza.
It gets lots of laughs—especially the stanza about "P.U."

Hum.
Get all your friends to join in.

Hold your nose,
make a face, and say, "P.U.!"
Fan the air away from your face,
and point to the kid in front of you.

On the last day of school,
lead your classmates in chanting:
"No more pencils!
No more books!
No more teachers'
dirty looks!"

Then, on your way out
the door, tell the teacher,
"Bet you're looking forward
to summer vacation this year.
But I'll sure miss you.
You're the best teacher
I've ever had."

Bruce Lansky

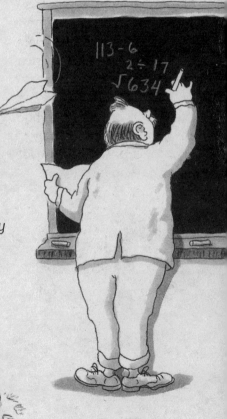

How to Torture Your Students

Start each day with a surprise quiz. Don't dismiss the class for recess until you've finished the lesson you're working on. At the end of the day, hand out a huge assignment that's due the next day.

When a student says, "I have to go to the bathroom," say, "You should have gone this morning before you left home" or "You'll have to hold it in; it's time for the kindergarten to use the bathrooms."

Never call on students who have their hands up. Only call on students who have no idea what's going on.

When a student asks you a question, say, "Look up the answer in a book." Don't bother to mention the name of the book in which the answer can be found.

When you read, go as fast as you can. Skip a line or two, then ask questions about the passage to see if the students were listening.

When it's time for the students to read, call on someone who doesn't have a book.

When you hand out pencils, make sure they're dull and don't have erasers. When you hand out books, make sure they're torn and tattered.

When preparing the students for a test, write all the information they'll need to know on the board. Then stand in front of the board so they can't see what you've written. As soon as you've finished discussing the test information, turn quickly and erase the board.

On the last day of school, hand out a surprise final exam. Tell your students if they flunk it, they'll have to attend summer school—and if they flunk summer school, they'll have to repeat the grade. Tell them you hope they all flunk because you like them so much and you wish they could be your students again next year.

Jane Pomazal and Bruce Lansky

The Story Behind the Poem: I once visited a school in Illinois, where a teacher had written a poem about how teachers can torture kids. I thought it was funny and expanded it. Now when I visit schools, it gets lots of laughs—especially from teachers.

Homework! Oh, Homework!

Homework! Oh, homework!
I hate you! You stink!
I wish I could wash you
away in the sink,
if only a bomb
would explode you to bits.
Homework! Oh, homework!
You're giving me fits.

I'd rather take baths
with a man-eating shark,
or wrestle a lion
alone in the dark,
eat spinach and liver,
pet ten porcupines,
than tackle the homework
my teacher assigns.

Homework! Oh, homework!
You're last on my list,
I simply can't see
why you even exist,
if you just disappeared
it would tickle me pink.
Homework! Oh, homework!
I hate you! You stink!

Jack Prelutsky

My Teacher Sees Right Through Me

I didn't do my homework.
My teacher asked me, "Why?"
I answered him, "It's much
   too hard."
He said, "You didn't try."

I told him, "My dog ate it."
He said, "You have no dog."
I said, "I went out running."
He said, "You never jog."

I told him, "I had chores to do."
He said, "You watched TV."
I said, "I saw the doctor."
He said, "You were with me."

My teacher sees right through
   my fibs,
which makes me very sad.
It's hard to fool the teacher
when the teacher is your dad.

Bruce Lansky

The Story Behind the Poem: My mother was a school librarian, and I'm glad I didn't attend the school where she taught. None of my excuses would have worked. She would have seen right through me.

Sick Day

I'm feeling sick and getting worse.
I think I'd better see the nurse.
I'm sure I should go home today.
It could be fatal if I stay.
I'm nauseated, nearly ill.
I have a fever and a chill.
I have a cold. I have the flu.
I'm turning green and pink and blue.
I have the sweats. I have the shakes,
a stuffy nose, and bellyaches.
My knees are weak. My vision's blurred.
My throat is sore. My voice is slurred.
I'm strewn with head lice, ticks, and mites.
I'm covered in mosquito bites.
I have a cough, a creak, a croak,
a reddish rash from poison oak,
a feeble head, a weakened heart.
I may just faint or fall apart.
I sprained my ankle, stubbed my toes,
and soon I'll start to decompose.
And one more thing I have today
that makes me have to go away.
It's just as bad as all the rest:
I also have a science test.

Kenn Nesbitt

A Sick-Day Trick

I didn't want to go to school,
and so I played a trick.
I coughed and wheezed and
  blew my nose
so Mom thought I was sick.

I slowly walked downstairs and lay
across the kitchen table.
When Mom said, "Sit up straight,"
I sighed, "I would, if I were able."

She looked at me a bit surprised
but felt my cheeks and head.
I told her I'd feel better
if I read a book in bed.

Mom sort of laughed, but
  soon agreed
to keep me home. Hooray!
There's just one thing that I forgot—
today is Saturday!

A. Maria Plover

My Parents Are Pretending

I'm pretty sure my parents are
pretending they are sick.
I know because I taught them both
to do that little trick.

You blow your nose and hold your head
and claim your brain is breaking.
And so, a pro like me would know
my folks are clearly faking.

A little thing I learned in school
convinced me I am right.
My parents are supposed to meet
my principal tonight.

Ted Scheu

Being Good?

My Teacher Pays Me to Be Good

My teacher pays me to be good,
Which I think is okay.
I get a dollar every time
I'm good for one whole day.

Whenever I behave myself
For one entire week,
He pays me twenty bucks and I'm
So happy I can't speak.

If I act proper for a month,
My teacher is so nice.
I get a hundred dollars for
My noble sacrifice.

And now my teacher says that if
I'm good throughout the year,
I'll get a trip to Disneyland.
It's lots of fun, I hear.

My teacher sold his car and moved
Out of our neighborhood.
He's running out of money,
But our class is really good.

Pat Dodds

Grateful acknowledgment is made to the following for permission to publish the copyrighted material listed below:

"Camera Phone," "DVD Report," "My Teacher Loves Her iPod," "My Teacher Sees Right Through Me," and "The Virus Cure," by Bruce Lansky. Copyright © 2005 by Bruce Lansky. Printed by permission of the author.

"Bring Your Own Lunch" by Bruce Lansky from *My Dog Ate My Homework!* Copyright © 1996, 2000 by Bruce Lansky. Reprinted by permission of Meadowbrook Press.

"How to Torture Your Teacher," "I Should Have Studied," "Too Busy," and "What I Found in My Desk" by Bruce Lansky from *No More Homework! No More Tests!: Kids' Favorite Funny School Poems*. Copyright © 1997 by Bruce Lansky. Reprinted by permission of Meadowbrook Press.

"Afterschool Snack" by Neal Levin from *Rolling in the Aisles: A Collection of Laugh-Out-Loud Poems*. Copyright © 2004 by Neal Levin. Reprinted by permission of Meadowbrook Press.

"Homework, I Love You," "I Can't Wait for Summer," "I'm Getting Sick of Peanut Butter," "I'm Practicing Telepathy," "Sick Day," and "When the Teacher Isn't Looking" by Kenn Nesbitt from *When the Teacher Isn't Looking: And Other Funny School Poems*. Copyright © 2005 by Kenn Nesbitt. Reprinted by permission of Meadowbrook Press.

"A Sick-Day Trick" by A. Maria Plover from *If Kids Ruled the School: More Kids' Favorite Funny School Poems*. Copyright © 2004 by A. Maria Plover. Reprinted by permission of Meadowbrook Press.

"How to Torture Your Students," by Jane Pomazal and Bruce Lansky from *If Kids Ruled the School: More Kids' Favorite Funny School Poems*. Copyright © 2004 by Jane Pomazal and Bruce Lansky. Reprinted by permission of Meadowbrook Press.

"I Ripped My Pants at School Today" by Robert Pottle from *MOXIE DAY and Family*. Copyright © 2002 by Robert Pottle. Reprinted by permission of Blue Lobster Press.

"Homework! Oh, Homework!" from *The New Kid on the Block*. Copyright © 1984 Jack Prelutsky. Used with the permission of Greenwillow Books, an imprint of HarperCollins Children's Books.

"My Parents Are Pretending," by Ted Scheu from *Rolling in the Aisles: A Collection of Laugh-Out-Loud Poems*. Copyright © 2004 by Ted Scheu. Reprinted by permission of Meadowbrook Press.

"Fs Are 'Fabulous'" by Ted Scheu from *If Kids Ruled the School: More Kids' Favorite Funny School Poems*. Copyright © 2004 by Ted Scheu. Reprinted by permission of Meadowbrook Press.

"My Teacher Pays Me to Be Good" by Pat Dodds by *If Kids Ruled the School: More Kids' Favorite Funny School Poems*. Copyright © 2004 by Pat Dodds. Reprinted by permission of Meadowbrook Press.